I Don't Want to go to Bed

By: Sarah Jane Rigby

I

Dedication

For Connor, Ayrton and Inés. You can achieve anything you want in life if you have the courage to dream it.

2

4

5

When dad calls out "**It's time for a bath!**" I run inside, then stop and laugh. So many bubbles to climb in between, when I am done I'll be **squeaky clean**.

8

12

Breathe **in** for
1 2 3 4
and **out** for
1 2 3 4

"Place your palms together and stretch your hands up high, as you inhale through your nose shape a mountain in the sky. **Now exhale** through your mouth, keeping your hands together bring them down level to your chest. **Soon you will be feeling less stressed.**"

18

"Going to bed can be nice,
if you listen to my advice.
A `story massage` will help
you to relax and unwind as
you remember what you
are **grateful** for today
in your mind."

19

Think happy thoughts as **you** close your eyes and sleep tight until sunrise.

Massage techniques

Olivia Owl is very clever, she knows what to do.
Eddie Elephant is good at remembering.
Marcus Meerkat keeps you safe and happy, he's always on the lookout for danger. This part of your brain doesn't understand language, but you can control it with breathing techniques and touch, through massage. When our Meerkat part of the brain feels overwhelmed and stressed we need to send it more oxygen to help us feel calm. We can do this by taking deep and slow breaths. Practicing breathing daily can help Marcus Meerkat know what to do. **Practicing story massage daily can help you to de-stress and relax and have fun and enjoyable quality time. Always ask permission before giving a story massage. Massage through clothes on the back as the child sits in front of you.**

Weather report:

"The sun is shining"- Use both hands flat on the upper part of the child's back to make circular movements. "It's starting to rain"- Use your fingers to gently tap. Start from the childs head and work your way down their back. "Now it's getting windy"- Use your hands flat and make big circles. "Lightning is striking"- Use your hand flat to make zigzag movements on the child's back. "And thunder is rumbling"- With the side of your hand gently use a chopping motion on the back and shoulders. "What do we see when we have rain and sunshine? A rainbow"- Start from the middle of the child's back and move your hands up and over the shoulders and down the arms.

Make a pizza:

"First we knead the dough, knead until its soft"- Use both hands flat on the upper part of the child's back to make circular movements, moving up to massage the shoulders. "Then we use a rolling pin and roll it to the top"- Use your forearm to roll up the child's back. "Now stretch it wide"- Use alternate hands and make big movements across the back. "And into a circle"- Make a big circle. "Now for the tomato sauce, spread it all around"- Use your hand, start at the top and move right to left as you spread down the back. "Sprinkle on the cheese"- Use your fingers to sprinkle as you start on the child's head and move down the back. "Now a bit of sweetcorn"- Tap the back with your fingers. "Let's chop up the ham"- Use the side of your hands and gently make chopping motions. "It's ready to go in the oven"- Start at the bottom of the back and slide your hands up the back to the top. "Now it's ready to eat, cut the pizza into slices"- Use the side of your hands to slide across diagonally.

Printed in Great Britain
by Amazon

27989084R00016